HERE COMES MR.
FLAT!

JAUME COPONS AND
LILIANA FORTUNY

Translated from the French by David Warriner

CRACKBOOM!

1

What a day!

"Tidy your room, or I'll throw away everything that's not in its place!" yells my mom.

I've barely been up for five minutes, and already my mom's screeching her famous "tidy your room" song. I can hear her from the kitchen, where I'm eating breakfast. I smile, because I just found the best thing to say to her.

"Okay, mom, I'll tidy it right away if you like!"

Of course, she doesn't say anything. We both know it's time to go to school.

"I'll tidy it when I get home," I say, as she grumbles away.

Actually, my mom's obsession about me tidying my room doesn't make any sense. As a matter of fact, my room isn't as untidy as she says it is. Well, that's what I think anyway.

After the hassle from my mom at breakfast time, it doesn't get any better at school. I've only been in the classroom five minutes before I realize all my classmates have a blue folder, and I don't.

Finally, Lidia explains that the teacher asked us to hand in all of our written assignments for the whole semester. But... when did she say that? And how come I don't know anything about it? This kind of thing happens to me all the time. And Lidia, who always knows what's going on, seems pretty smug to see me taken by surprise.

I have to say, the worst thing about Lidia is not that she's an annoying know-it-all who loves to see other people mess up (and especially me). The very worst thing of all is that we're neighbors. And not only do we live in the same apartment building, we even live on the same floor! It's terrible, because every time Lidia sees my mom, she tells her EVERYTHING. Everything I should have done and didn't and everything I shouldn't have done but did.

What a day! First my mom screeching her song about tidying my room, now Lidia and the written assignments. But that's not the end of it! Two minutes later, Emma the school librarian walks into our classroom. Before she even opens her mouth, I know it's me she wants to talk to.

The day before, I played hide-and-seek during recess. And I hid in the library. When my friends came in looking for me, I ran out before they could see me. And without meaning to, I knocked some books off the shelves. I figured I would go back and put them away later, but I forgot.

As I fear, I have to go with Emma to the library. I'm surprised to see the books have been tidied away, though. I'm relieved she's not making me do it myself, but her twisted mind has surely dreamed up some much more severe punishment for me.

My job involves putting a whole bunch of books into cardboard boxes. Then I have to stack those boxes up by the door. It's so unfair!

I've been working in the storeroom for a while. Do you have any idea how heavy a box full of books can be?! And there's not just one of them, oh no! There are two, three, four, five … and as I'm packing the sixth box I notice some kind of furry orange stuffed toy, neither big nor small. Even though it's covered in dust, I think it's pretty cute. It has a wide mouth and big eyes. If it could walk on all fours, it would look a bit like a cat or a dog. But the way it's lying, it looks more like a funny little yeti or something, or … a monster.

When I've finished packing and stacking the boxes, I call Emma over. I have to say that she is very happy with my work. I ask her who the stuffed creature belongs to.

It was already lying there, dying of boredom, when I started working at the library.
Do you want to keep it?

Why would I want some stuffie for babies? What would I do with a little dust-magnet like that?
But okay, I suppose, rather than leave it here on its own …

Of course I want it!

SCRATCH
SCRATCH
SCRATCH

Thanks, Emma.

Five minutes later, I'm back in the classroom, but I have to wait until the others get back from recess. I quickly stuff the creature into my bag. The last thing I want is for the others to laugh at me and ask what I'm doing with an orange stuffie.

I'm happy because it's Friday and I can stay at home in peace for the next two days. I think my troubles are behind me, but I'm wrong. Just as I'm stepping out the door to leave, the teacher calls me back.

I forgot! This weekend the school is celebrating its 25th birthday. There's a party on Sunday for all the students. I have no other choice if I want to get it all done. I have to go home and write non-stop until the party on Sunday. Phew, what a day!

2

What an evening!

As soon as I get home, I go into the kitchen to see my parents. I tell them I want to lock myself in my room until the school party. Why? For one simple reason: I have a whole bunch of homework to do. For a moment, this takes them completely by surprise. It's the first time in my life I've ever talked to them about homework. But they seem okay with it.

When I get to my room, I realize there's no way I can work right away. There's way too much stuff on my desk. So, with a sweep of my arm I clear all the clutter off the desktop. That way I'll have a nice clean surface to do my homework on. Then I have an idea. Maybe if I dig around in my closet I'll find some of my written assignments in there. I did do the work during the year, but I must have misplaced it all. I have no idea where.

Yes, I've found one! I've found one of my written assignments! I decide to read it through because I wrote it a long time ago and I don't really remember what it's about. Okay, and maybe because I should make sure it's good enough to hand in as well.

> Once upon a time, there was a day that wanted to be the night. Because that was impossible, the day chose to become a stormy day instead. You know, the kind of day that almost looks like night.

> Well, I've heard better, but that story's not bad!

I feel like I can hear a voice somewhere, but I don't really pay much attention to it.

> One day, a solar eclipse made the sky go very, very dark. And so, the day found out, completely by chance, what it felt like to be as dark as the night.

> Ooh, now it's getting interesting!

I hear the voice again. I figure it's just my dad walking past my room trying to tell me something.

This time I can hear the voice clearly. I know it's strange, but it sounds like it's coming from my backpack.

Suddenly I see it. It's emerging from my bag and shaking the dust off its fur. I can't believe my eyes! Is it an alien? An elf? A... monster? I don't know what to say. I'm so surprised, I'm lost for words.

After these introductions, the book monster starts to tell me how, to stay awake, he has to read and listen to a good story. If he doesn't, he goes into hibernation and turns back into a stuffie. That's how I found him in the library storeroom. It's hard to believe. But what's really amazing is what happens right afterward. This mini-monster breaks into song and starts dancing. Wait, he's telling me all about himself!

I'M MR. FLAT, AND
I'M FREE AT LAST!

I DON'T KNOW HOW,
I DON'T KNOW WHY,
I DON'T KNOW WHERE OR WHEN,
I WAS CHASED OUT OF A BOOK,
AND THEN I GOT STUCK.

I'M THE BOOK MONSTER!
GOOD STORIES BRING ME TO LIFE!
FUN STORIES, EXCITING TALES,
READ ME STORIES BIG AND SMALL,
I DON'T CARE, I LOVE THEM ALL!

I'M MR. FLAT, AND
I'M FREE AT LAST!

When he's done singing, Mr. Flat asks me again if I have any books. So I show him where they are, and he feasts his eyes on all of them. Then one of the titles catches his attention. He picks *Treasure Island* off the shelf.

"What a super story!" he says. "Come on then, my boy, let's get going! I was stuck in that storeroom far too long! I need a good story. Right now. Let's read!"

As I'm about to start reading, Mr. Flat starts jumping around on my bed. He's so happy. And it's hard for me not to feel happy too!

I start reading the first chapter, but Mr. Flat interrupts and asks me to read the epigraph. The what? I hadn't even noticed there was something written at the front of the book. It's not easy for me to understand, but the words certainly leave an impression on me.

There's very little I find more moving than Stevenson's epigraph in *Treasure Island*!

TO THE HESITATING PURCHASER

To the Hesitating Purchaser
If sailor tales to sailor tunes,
Storm and adventure, heat and cold,
If schooners, islands, and maroons,
And buccaneers, and buried gold,
And all the old romance, retold,
Exactly in the ancient way,
Can please, as me they pleased of old,
The wiser youngsters of today:

—So be it, and fall on! If not,
If studious youth no longer crave,
His ancient appetites forgot,
Kingston, or Ballantyne the Brave,
Or Cooper of the wood and wave:

So be it, also! And may I
And all my pirates share the grave
Where these and their creations lie!

R. L. STEVENSON

* Robert Louis Stevenson, *Treasure Island*, 1883

I read to him for a long time. I've never read aloud for so long in my whole life. Every now and then, Mr. Flat stands up to act out (and exaggerate) what I'm reading. He limps like a pirate with a wooden leg. And when one of the characters jumps up, he jumps up too. I can't stop laughing. Mr. Flat is just too funny! But then before I know it, I have to stop reading. It's dinner time!

3

A good night after a bad day!

Just like every Friday night, we have pizza for dinner. I like to add a personal touch to mine. Tonight, my little extra is a fried egg. Yum! I devour my whole plate in three minutes flat. Before I've finished chewing my last mouthful, I get up from the table and tell my parents I'm going back to my room.

No, it's not because I can't wait to do my homework or tidy my room. How can you even think about homework or cleanup when you've just met a monster? Back in my room, I lie down on my bed, and Mr. Flat and I keep on reading.

Mr. Flat is right. Sometimes going back to a place I love makes me appreciate it even more. I figure the same must be true for reading books as well.

Mr. Flat picks out another book, *Peter Pan*. I open it and start reading.

"All children, except one, grow up. They soon know that they will grow up ..."

"Ah, how I've missed Peter and Wendy!" says Mr. Flat. "Captain Hook, Smee, and the crew ... Barrie really knew his stuff."

"Barrie?"

"Yes, James Barrie, the author of the book! Did you know that before it became a book, *Peter Pan* was a play?"

No, I didn't know that. But I'm starting to see how all these books I've always found really boring are way more interesting than I thought.

As strange as it might seem, a misunderstanding between Peter Pan and Wendy makes Peter think a thimble is the same thing as a kiss!

As we are reading, I feel like Mr. Flat and I are floating in the clouds, over the rooftops, to Neverland, just like Peter, Wendy, and her brothers.

We read *Peter Pan* for a good while until Mr. Flat asks me to start reading another book. Like I did for *Treasure Island*, I mark the page we got to before I close the book. I know I'll find the time to keep reading where we left off. This time, Mr. Flat chooses *The Adventures of Tom Sawyer*, by Mark Twain.

"One of my favourite parts is when Tom Sawyer has to paint the garden fence as punishment," Mr. Flat says. "He cleverly persuades his friends to do the job for him by making them think painting a fence is a really fun thing to do!"

But what I find strange is why a man with such a simple name as Samuel Langhorne Clemens would rather go by the name of Mark Twain. Writers certainly do some strange things sometimes!

Later, Mr. Flat asks me to switch books again. I figure now's a good time to ask him a question that's been running through my mind.

HOW WE WERE BANISHED FROM
THE BOOK OF MONSTERS
TOLD BY Mr. Flat

"One day, a man named Dr. Brut came into *The Book of Monsters* with his sidekick, Nabo. He wheedled his way in and made friends with all the monsters. We all really liked him at first."

"But Dr. Brut tricked us. One night, he invited us all to dinner to celebrate his birthday. Then, when we woke up the next day, we weren't in the book anymore."

"We don't know why he did it. And we don't know why he hated us so much. Nobody knows why Dr. Brut is so mean."

Mr. Flat's story makes me feel very sad. I figure I should help him.

REASONS WHY I FIGURE I SHOULD HELP Mr. Flat

1. He seems like a good person, or rather, a good monster.
2. It's unfair that he was banished from his own book.
3. It's obvious that Dr. Brut is a very bad man.
4. I haven't known Mr. Flat for very long, but he already feels like my friend.
5. Mr. Flat didn't deserve what happened to him.

That night, we fall asleep reading together. The last thing I remember is reading some of *The Wind in the Willows* by Kenneth Grahame, which is kind of about a mole and a rat walking around in the howling wind. I think I even felt the wind on my face. I remember Mr. Flat raving about the illustrations by Ernest Howard Shepard, too.

Mr. Flat and I are already sound asleep (well, mostly) when my dad comes into my room to turn out the light. I open my eye a tiny bit and prick up my ears, enough to see the look on his face and hear what he says.

4

Alex and the book monster

First I open one eye, then the other. For a moment, I watch the light streaming through the slats of my window blind. I take a deep breath. Suddenly, I start to worry "What if …" What if this happened, and what if that happened…

SOME OF THE "WHAT IFS" I CAN'T STOP WORRYING ABOUT

What if Mr. Flat isn't here anymore?

What if he doesn't really exist?

What if it was all my imagination?

What if I'm going crazy?

What if he is just a stuffie, after all?

I'm afraid to turn over in case Mr. Flat isn't there anymore. Fortunately, I can hear a gentle snoring sound. Phew, he is here! It really is him. He's just asleep!

I feel a bit sheepish because asking someone who's sleeping whether they're asleep is kind of a silly thing to do.

To make up for waking him, I tell Mr. Flat about an idea that's crossed my mind. If he likes, every week I can borrow some books from the school library and bring them home. That way, we can read them together.

Perfect, Alex.
I love books…

About sailors…

About pirates…

And adventurers…

About magicians…

And knights…

Because Mr. Flat and I are awake early, we stay in my bed and read for a while. When we're done, he tells me the story of a man who, according to Baron Munchausen, was the world's fastest runner. Mr. Flat illustrates this by tearing across my room, leaving a cloud of orange behind him.

Before he stops running, the door suddenly opens. Mr. Flat slams on the brakes and screeches to a halt in the middle of my room, where he stands as still as a stuffie. My dad comes into the room.

While I'm eating breakfast, my dad reminds me why I have to go to school. A few weeks ago, I signed up for a basketball tournament to celebrate the school's 25th birthday. He says I have to go.

My parents have it all planned out! My dad and I will be at school while my mom does the groceries. She'll come by and meet us there later. But what about Mr. Flat? What am I supposed to do with Mr. Flat?

There's no way I can convince Mr. Flat to come to school. He would rather stay at home. I realize he's quite stubborn. When he makes a decision, he doesn't change his mind. Before we leave, I have to find my gym gear. It's not easy, but I find it in the end.

On the way to school, my dad gives me a little speech. He loves speeches.

I'm the last one to get there. My teammates are waiting excitedly by the school entrance. There are only five minutes to go until the tournament begins.

As soon as the game starts, I realize my teammates are being overoptimistic. Our opponents are taller and stronger than we are, and they play better than we do!

Unfortunately, we don't catch up. It's the worst game I've played in my entire life, and believe me, I've played some bad ones. We don't even score a single basket. Fahrenheit Academy are just too good. They barely give us time to catch our breath!

There is an upside to our defeat, though. Since we're eliminated from the tournament, I can go home now and get back to Mr. Flat!

I'm raring to go, keen to get home right after the game, but then that strange phenomenon occurs where your mom or dad starts talking to the other parents and there's no way you can get them to budge. I do manage to pry my dad away, but it's hard work. Then I have to endure another speech from my dad about patience and why it's important for kids to learn to wait.

My dad finally understands that I have to finish my work. We walk home, telling ourselves we'll probably cross paths with my mom anyway. My dad seizes the opportunity to give me another one of his little speeches.

5

Where is Mr. Flat?

Back at home, I go straight to my room. There's a terrible surprise waiting for me. My room is tidy! Well, that's not a terrible surprise in itself. The real surprise is that Mr. Flat isn't here anymore! He's nowhere to be seen!

I have a bad feeling. A very bad feeling. I'm sure my mom has followed through with her threat and has thrown away everything I left lying around. I feel like the rug's been pulled out from under me.

I hurry to the kitchen, where I find two bags full of my stuff right where my parents usually put the garbage before they carry it out to the dumpster. Without hesitation, I start to dig through the bags. I find a lot of things in there, but not Mr. Flat.

SOME OF THE THINGS I FIND IN THE GARBAGE

- Math and English notes
- Half a watch strap
- A few little sketches I did
- Three pens and a pencil
- A yoyo without a string
- A piece of leftover croissant
- A videogame magazine

- A baseball hat
- A gym sock
- A pair of remote-control car wheels
- Some drawings of planes
- The lenses from my old sunglasses

My legs are shaking, and I start to feel the same kind of lump in my throat I get when I'm about to cry. Suddenly, I hear the front door open. I rush over, sure it's my mom getting home. Yes, it's her!

Because I'm very insistent, my mom tells me a long nightmare of a story that I'll sum up in three key points so it doesn't drag on.

THREE KEY POINTS OF THE NIGHTMARE STORY MY MOM TELLS ME

While my mom was tidying my room, she remembered that the older kids at school were having a secondhand toy sale to raise money for their end-of-year school trip.

Without hesitation, she grabbed Mr. Flat and everything else that was lying around and took it to the toy sale.

Poor Mr. Flat was abandoned there with a bunch of other stuffies, old toys, and all kinds of weird things like frog-shaped teacups.

I feel my blood boiling! I'm not sure how exactly, but I manage to convince my dad to walk me to school again. Before we set off, I go back to my room and use a knife to pry open my piggy bank. I empty every last penny out of it. Whatever it takes, I'm going to buy back Mr. Flat and bring him home again!

When we get to school, I rush over to the toy table. There are all kinds of strange objects there, but there's no sign of Mr. Flat.

That's when I notice some girls from my class standing around the drinking fountain in the schoolyard. I hurry over to them, sure that one of them must have bought Mr. Flat.

My classmates tell me Lidia's gone home. For the first time in my life, I tell myself it's a stroke of good luck that Lidia and I live on the same floor! All I have to do is tear my dad away from school again so we can go home!

Of course, my dad gives me another one of his speeches on the way home. But honestly, this time I can't remember what he's going on about.

I don't follow my dad back into our apartment right away. I stay out in the hallway and knock on Lidia's door instead. Her dad, Mr. Lines, opens the door. He's just as annoying as his daughter, if not more. What really annoys me is how he always calls me "champ." Champ here, champ there, champ this, champ that. Ugh!

I tell Lidia's dad I'll come back at seven o'clock, and then I go home. I'm furious he would think I wanted to ask Lidia whether we had any homework to hand in on Monday. However, I'm so worried about Mr. Flat, I don't give it a second thought. I don't feel well. I told Mr. Flat I would help him find his book, and all I've managed to do is lose him! I'm exhausted. I realize just how exhausted I am when I catch sight of myself in the mirror at home.

MY REFLECTION IN THE MIRROR

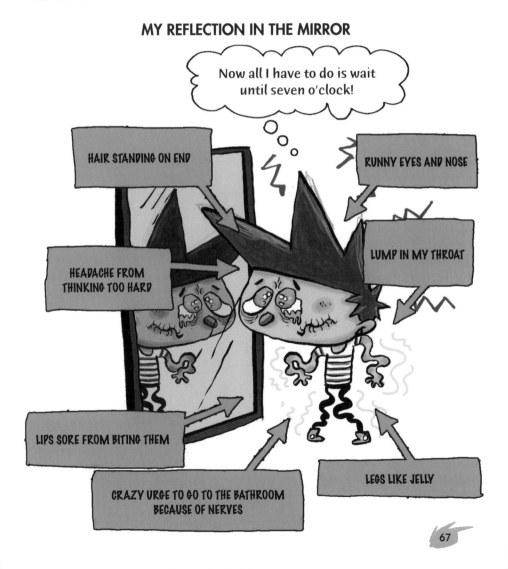

6

Ticktock, ticktock…

I shut myself into my room again, on the pretext of doing my homework. I do have time to write a few assignments, but I can't think about that right now. All I can think about is Mr. Flat. In Lidia's hands, anything might happen to him. The girl next door sure is good at doing her homework, but who knows how she'll react if Mr. Flat starts talking to her!

Possible reaction A

Possible reaction B

Possible reaction C

I feel sad, I feel worried, and I feel very angry at my mom, but I'm even angrier at myself. If only I had tidied my room a little bit, even just a tiny bit!

Seriously, the time is going by far too slowly. To pass the time, I pick up *Twenty Thousand Leagues Under the Sea*, by Jules Verne.

Just a few pages in, I can already feel the solitude of the ocean floor setting in. I can hear the creaking wood of sinking boats. I notice the quick, exaggerated movements of sharks swimming by. I can sense the speed of the submarine Nautilus, and I can feel the terror of being attacked by a giant squid. But what resonates the most with me is the boredom Ned the harpooner feels, and the pain Captain Nemo struggles with throughout the long voyage.

Lunch time!

Time to eat, Alex!

Alex, lunch is ready!

I take a short break to eat my lunch. My parents feed me through a funnel so I can get back to my room quickly and keep reading the Jules Verne story.

I hope you didn't really think I ate through a funnel. That's just my way of saying I ate super-quickly!

Alex, are you trying to beat the world speed-eating record?

My, you are in a hurry!

I just have to finish my homework!

And so I go back to my room to keep reading, together with Captain Nemo, Ned the tall harpooner, and all the other characters in the story. But around five o'clock, my eyelids start to feel heavy.

That's right, I fall asleep. Fast asleep. I don't even realize I'm dozing off! I have a bad dream, or a good dream, or a good bad dream, depending on how you look at it.

In my dream, I'm at the bottom of the sea. Even though I'm underwater, I can still breathe easily, somehow. I can hear music, and I can smell something a little minty. It's quite dark, and I can't see much, but I stay relatively calm. I'm not scared at all. I see a very strange submarine float by. The passengers on board give me a friendly wave.

Suddenly, I feel like someone's right behind me. But when I turn around, there's nobody there. The same thing happens three or four times, until I turn around really quickly and see all kinds of little monsters looking at me.

They don't say anything, they just nod their heads and smile. Then I hear a familiar voice, a very familiar voice, as clear as day!

Luckily, the voice I hear is my dad's. He's come to wake me up because I told him I had to be at Lidia's at seven o'clock, no matter what.

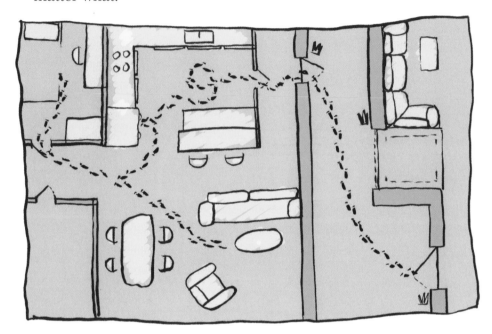

I grab the money I found earlier in my piggy bank and stuff it into my pocket. Then I take a deep breath and make my way over to Lidia's. It's not far at all, but it's a very important journey.

7

Negotiating with Lidia Lines

The moment of truth is finally here! All I have to do is knock at the door, talk to Lidia, and get Mr. Flat back. I'm prepared to buy him back for the price she paid, no problem. However, I'm greeted by an unpleasant surprise. It's her annoying dad who opens the door.

What a silly question! Of course I want him to fetch Lidia! Why else would I be knocking at the door? And that habit of calling me "champ" is really starting to bug me!

Lidia and her dad are just as bad as each other! I try to keep my cool as I tell Lidia the story of Mr. Flat. But I don't tell her the true story, just a story I make up as I go along.

I tell her Mr. Flat was my first stuffie and that I love him very much.

I also tell her I can't go to sleep without him.

I tell her how my mom thought I didn't want him anymore...

82

At the end of my story, Lidia doesn't say a word. That's one of the most horrible things that can happen, when you tell a story and there's no reaction. Eventually, because I don't say anything either, she has no choice but to say something. That's almost worse than the silence.

I'm outraged. Not only did she change his name to something as ludicrous as Blabi, but she lost him as well! And that doesn't seem to bother her in the slightest. As she tells me what happened, I have to bite my tongue to stop myself from screaming!

LIDIA LINES'S EXPLANATION

My aunt and I went to school and bought Blabi.

Then we went shopping and ate lunch.

In the afternoon, we went to a movie. Later, when we came out of the movie theater, I noticed Blabi wasn't there anymore.

My aunt said it didn't matter, because Blabi was just a grubby old stuffie. She bought me another one instead.

Lidia is the queen of annoying people. I won't even say a word about her aunt! How could she say Mr. Flat was old and grubby? As if that really mattered! But Lidia still hasn't really given me an answer.

Lidia runs off to her room and comes back with a horrible stuffed chihuahua. She holds it out proudly for me to admire. That must be the stuffie her aunt bought for her!

I have so many questions, my head is spinning.

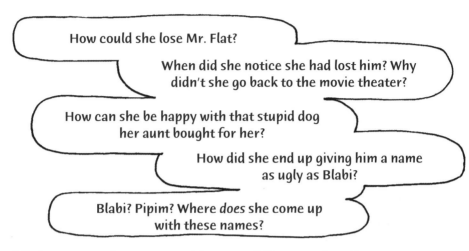

> How could she lose Mr. Flat?

> When did she notice she had lost him? Why didn't she go back to the movie theater?

> How can she be happy with that stupid dog her aunt bought for her?

> How did she end up giving him a name as ugly as Blabi?

> Blabi? Pipim? Where *does* she come up with these names?

All these questions are making me fall apart, but I manage to pull myself together. I've put my finger on the question I know I have to ask her.

> Listen, Lidia, I have a lot of questions, but the most important one is...

> Can you tell me which movie theater you were at?

> The Victoria!

I forget all about Lidia in a heartbeat. For a fraction of a second, I see all kinds of unthinkable scenarios scrolling by before my eyes. Here are the worst ones:

He gets run down by a car when he is crossing the street.

A dog runs off with him in its jaws.

He falls into the formidable Dr. Brut's hands.

But that only lasts a fraction of a second before I run off down the stairs. By the time Lidia realizes what's happened, I'm already at the bottom of the stairwell.

Alex, you're so rude! You didn't even said hello to Pipim!

8

Searching
for Mr. Flat

I might not be very good at basketball, but nobody's faster than me at running down stairs. It's like I'm jumping from one level to the next, and for a second I feel just like Peter Pan. I make it down to the ground floor quicker than if I were flying.

I'm so fired up when I step outside onto the sidewalk that I look in both directions, even though I know the Victoria movie theater is to the right. I only start to calm down when I see the lights of the movie theater sign in the distance. I'm running so quickly, I'm sure I'd make the world's fastest man from Baron Munchausen's book of travels look like he's standing still.

I don't even realize how much I'm running. Apparently, I run right by Emma the librarian (the next day, at school, she tells me she saw me running down the street like a madman). I also run right past a store window full of toy dogs like Lidia's. All just as horrible, of course. I run so fast, I trip and bang my head on a streetlamp, but I'm in such a hurry I get right up again and keep on running.

In no time at all, I'm standing in front of the Victoria! It used to be one big movie theater, but they converted it into a multiplex. People are walking out of the theater. I stay right there by the front door to see if anyone has happened to find Mr. Flat, but I'm not so lucky.

When everyone has finally left, I ask the lady at the ticket office if anyone has found an orange stuffie. She tells me all she does is sell the tickets. She doesn't know anything about the lost-and-found. In fact, nobody knows anything at all.

I check all ten theaters at the Victoria, one by one. I look on the floor, under the seats and in the garbage. I look everywhere, but I'm not very lucky at all. I'm about to admit defeat. I've failed so miserably! I promised Mr. Flat I'd help him find *The Book of Monsters*. I feel terrible just thinking about it. I've done such a bad job of not losing him! I really don't feel well. It feels like a ton of bad luck is raining down on me.

As if I'd finished last in a race.

As if we were having my least-favorite food for dinner.

As if I'd been given a horrible present and I had to pretend I liked it.

As if someone had dumped a bucket of ice-cold water over my head.

I'm about to walk away when the cleaning lady comes over to console me. I suppose she's sorry to see me so sad.

Actually, I would say there's nothing young about the man at the concession stand. I have a to wait for a moment before I talk to him, because there are some customers ordering popcorn and drinks.

I don't want any popcorn!

Nothing to drink, either.

Small, medium, or large popcorn?

Ah! Something to drink, then?

Tell me, why are you here then?

I tell him what I've already explained to the lady in the ticket office, the man who checks the tickets, and the cleaning lady.

I only started my shift ten minutes ago. Maybe a customer handed it in to the young man who was here before me. Sometimes, people find things under the seats and bring them here. We put them in the cloakroom out back. Follow me!

Suddenly, I feel hopeful again. I follow the young man from the concession stand (even though there's nothing young about him) through a door beside the washrooms.

It's crazy in here! There are jackets, coats, bags, cellphones, scarves, handkerchiefs, a motorcycle helmet, two hats, five sweaters. Everything you can imagine, in fact, except Mr. Flat.

My hope doesn't last long. I feel like I have a mountain on my shoulders. But as I retrace my steps, I hear a familiar voice that sounds like it's coming from a long way away.

Hey, what took you so long?!?

I can't believe it! I've found him! Mr. Flat is right at the bottom of this pile of lost things! He won't stop talking and keeps asking questions as he hugs me tight. I say only one thing to him, but I say it in all seriousness.

Where were you?

Does your mom often go on a cleaning rampage?

Now that we've found each other again, we can go home, right?

Don't you think now would be a great time to read a book? I haven't read anything for hours!

I'll never lose you again, Mr. Flat!

I know very well that one day, when we find *The Book of Monsters*, Mr. Flat and I will have to go our separate ways. But until then, I'll look after him and make sure nothing bad happens to him.

9

Back home again!

Home Sweet Home

After we thank the man at the concession stand, we go back home. People in the street must think it's a little strange for a boy my age to be clutching a stuffie, but I don't care, because I know Mr. Flat is no ordinary stuffie!

And who do we cross paths with in the hallway? That's right, Lidia Lines and her dad. It's like they're having a contest to see which one of them can be the most annoying. Lidia's question is absurd. If she can see I'm carrying Mr. Flat, then of course I found him! But it gets worse when her dad compares Mr. Flat to her horrible dog stuffie and says the dog is cuter!

The worst thing about Lidia and her dad is not that they are annoying. It is their never-ending questions. Mr. Flat and I can't wait to get home, but we have to listen to all of their questions first. And at the end of it all, Lidia asks me the million-dollar question that reminds me why I'm still not out of this whole mess!

We make it through the interrogation from Lidia and her dad, but soon my parents will be asking me the very same things. Before anything else, I take Mr. Flat back into my room. Then I go into the dining room to field my parents' questions. And they have lots! After the interrogation from Lidia and her dad, and the grilling from my mom and dad, I figure it must be National Question Day or something!

My parents ask me so many questions at once, I don't have a choice but to answer in one never-ending monologue. I end up telling a few white lies, of course, just to avoid having to answer even more questions.

Let's see. It was Emma, the school librarian, who gave me this stuffie as a good-luck charm. His name is Mr. Flat. That's why I don't want anyone else to touch him again. And if I have to keep my room tidy, then yes, I'll keep my room tidy.

Mr. Flat was at Lidia's place because Lidia bought him from the toy table at school. If you don't mind, I'm going to finish my homework in my room. It would be a shame if all these questions stopped me from getting it done.

Even I'm surprised how many white lies I manage to tell. I did have a good reason for telling them, though. Still, I don't get to escape so easily. My parents make me finish my dinner before they let me go back to my room. Soup, omelet, and yogurt. I wolf it all down in eight minutes flat. While we eat, I think about my written assignments. I'm going to run out of time. I never had any peace and quiet to get it all done. Too bad! At least I found Mr. Flat!

In case you didn't notice, here are the three biggest white lies I told my parents:

1. Of course, Mr. Flat isn't a good-luck charm.
2. I wasn't at Lidia's the whole time.
3. I'm not in any hurry at all to finish my homework. All I want to do is read with Mr. Flat.

After dinner, I go to my room. There I find Mr. Flat dancing and singing on top of a blue folder on my desk.

A-wop-bop-a-loo-bop-a-wop-bam-boom!

You took your time, Alex! Come on, open the folder! We have some work to do before we can read.

Mr. Flat wants me to open the blue folder on my desk. I do what he says, and I nearly faint in surprise. My written assignments are all there! When I ask him where he found them, he starts to dance again and sing me his answers.

Are you looking for a paper?
Then you never should waver!
And another paper?
Then do yourself a favor!
You need a little bit of magic
And a lot of hard work!

With not even a mark on the wall
Mr. Flat's found them all! (except one)

I'm Mr. Flat, and I'm free, free, free!
I'm the friendly book monster
and it's great to be free!

When he's done singing, Mr. Flat tells me not to get too excited. Even though we have the written assignment I found by myself (the one about the day that wanted to be the night) and all the assignments he found, there's still one missing: the one I was supposed to hand in on Friday. Without hesitation, I grab a sheet of paper and a pen, and I get to work.

As I'm trying to write my assignment, though, I can see that Mr. Flat is looking at me as if he's trying to tell me something.

And then something incredible happens. Mr. Flat opens the door to my closet and, suddenly, my room is filled with a whole bunch of monsters. Monsters of all shapes and all colors! There are MONSTERS, MONSTERS EVERYWHERE!!!

Mr. Flat introduces me to his friends, one by one. And the strange thing is, even though I'm meeting them for the first time, it feels like we've been friends forever.

After he introduces all the monsters to me, Mr. Flat introduces me to them, and I blush a little.

When the introductions are over, we all sit down on my bed. I'm worried about what my parents are going to think when they find all these monsters in my room.

No problem. We'll just pretend to be stuffies.

We won't move a muscle.

They won't suspect a thing.

Your parents will think we're stuffed toys.

You'll just have to play it by ear. You'll strike the right note.

Tell them you found us when you found Mr. Flat and you've been hiding us in your backpack or in your closet.

Call your parents!

So, I call my parents. As soon as they set foot in my room, they see all these monsters lined up nice and tidily on my shelf. They seem surprised to see I have so many stuffies, but they don't think there's anything wrong with it. I tell them Emma the librarian gave them to me when she gave me Mr. Flat.

So long as your room is tidy, you do what you want.

Well, I think they're horrible, but if you like them...